Pokémon DP is finally roaring into its Platinum version! In the Sinnoh Competition, a collection of new characters burst onto the scene in a free for-all battle! Will Hareta triumph over them all?

You'll also find a ton of special extras inside just for Pokémon fans like you! Hope you enjoy reading it as much as I enjoyed making it!

– *Shigekatsu Ihara*

Shigekatsu Ihara's other manga titles include *Pokémon: Lucario and the Mystery of Mew, Pokémon Emerald Challenge!!* and *Battle Frontier, Dual Jack!!*

Pokémon DIAMOND AND PEARL ADVENTURE!
Vol. 6
VIZ Kids Edition

Story & Art by **SHIGEKATSU IHARA**

Original Japanese edition
"Pokémon D•P POCKET MONSTER DIAMOND PEARL MONOGATARI"
published by SHOGAKUKAN Inc.

Translation/Kaori Inoue
Touch-up Art & Lettering/Eric Erbes
Graphics & Cover Design/Hitomi Yokoyama Ross
Editor/Annette Roman

VP, Production/Alvin Lu
VP, Sales & Product Marketing/Gonzalo Ferreyra
VP, Creative/Linda Espinosa
Publisher/Hyoe Narita

Printed in the U.S.A.

Published by VIZ Media, LLC
P.O. Box 77010
San Francisco, CA 94107

10 9 8 7 6 5 4 3 2 1
First printing, March 2010

vizkids
www.vizkids.com

www.viz.com

Volume 6

Story & Art by

MAIN CHARACTERS
HARETA
A WILD BOY WHO HAS A SPECIAL BOND WITH POKÉMON! HE'S MORE ENTHUSIASTIC ABOUT POKÉMON BATTLES THAN ANY OTHER TRAINER!
EMPOLEON
THIS IS THE POKÉMON PIPLUP AFTER TWO EVOLUTIONS. A FAITHFUL PARTNER WHO HAS STOOD BY HARETA THROUGH COUNTLESS BATTLES.
JUN
FRIENDS WITH HARETA AND MITSUMI. JUN'S A LITTLE STRANGE BUT HAS SOME SERIOUS TRAINER TALENT!
MITSUMI
PROFESSOR ROWAN'S ASSISTANT AND HARETA'S FRIEND. ONCE A TEAM GALACTIC COMMANDER, SHE IS REFORMED NOW.
PROFESSOR ROWAN
THE POKÉMON RESEARCHER WHO RAISED HARETA AND HAS HIGH HOPES FOR HARETA AS A TRAINER.

TEAM GALACTIC
AN EVIL ORGANIZATION THAT SEEKS TO EXPLOIT POKÉMON.

KOYA
A MYSTERIOUS YOUNG MAN WITH INCREDIBLE TRAINER SKILLS. HE IS COLD AND CALCULATING AND ALWAYS HAS A BATTLE PLAN.

CYNTHIA
FOUGHT ALONGSIDE HARETA AND THE OTHERS AT MOUNT CORONET AND IS LAST YEAR'S SINNOH COMPETITION CHAMPION.

THE STORY SO FAR

Hareta defeated Team Galactic in their quest to capture Dialga, the Ruler of Time. However, using the Red Chain, the Team Galactic leader summoned Palkia, the Ruler of Space. A massive battle between Dialga and Palkia caused a warp in space and time that swallowed our entire world in darkness! Thanks to Hareta's bravery, though, the two Pokémon went back to their individual realms, and peace returned to our world. But another battle is about to begin in Sinnoh...

TABLE OF CONTENTS

WINTER OUTFIT!

CHAPTER 1
A NEW BATTLE BEGINS!

IN THE AFTERMATH OF THE BATTLE ON MOUNT CORONET, PEACE SETTLES ACROSS SINNOH. UNTIL...
BAM
BOOM
HURRAY
CHEER
YAY
WOOT
THE CURTAIN RISES ON A *NEW ADVENTURE!*

ALL RIGHT!
WOW! LOOK AT ALL THESE FANS!
NO SURPRISE THERE. THIS COMPETITION DECIDES WHO THE NUMBER ONE TRAINER IN SINNOH IS GONNA BE!
TOO COOL!
DON'T WEAR YOURSELF OUT, HARETA!
REMEMBER, WE'RE PART OF THIS COMPETITION TOO!
WE PRACTICED AND BATTLED AND GOT ALL OUR BADGES...
AND NOW WE'RE STRONG ENOUGH TO KNOCK THEIR SOCKS OFF!
YEAH! LET'S GET THOSE SOCKS!
TOO EXCITED TO FOLLOW WHAT I'M SAYING, HUH?
YAAAAH
THANK YOU FOR YOUR PATIENCE...

HEY!
IT'S MITSUMI!
CHEEEEER
OUR FIRST BATTLE PITS MITSUMI AGAINST LAST YEAR'S CHAMPION, CYNTHIA!

HUSSSH

GO, MITSUMI! GO, CYNTHIA! I HOPE YOU BOTH WIN!
YAY!
AND I HOPE YOU UNDER-STAND THAT ONE OF THEM HAS TO LOSE!

WHEN I HEARD YOU ENTERED THE COMPETITION, I HAD THEM CHANGE THE TOURNAMENT CHART A WEE BIT. ♡
I JUST HAD TO FACE OFF AGAINST THE GIRL THEY CALL "TEAM GALACTIC'S FINEST."

AND I THINK IT'LL BE A LOT OF FUN BATTLING YOU.
ACTUALLY, IT'S KINDA SCARY!
GO EASY ON ME, OKAY, MS. CHAMPION?

NOW, LET'S GET READY TOOOO...

... BATTLE !
BAM

ZZB

THUD
CHARGE
INFERNAPE!
GARCHOMP!

OVERHEAT!
GIGA IMPACT!
BOOOM

WHOOOSH
WHAT THE...
I-INCREDIBLE! THEY'RE *STILL* AT IT!
CHEEER
THIS IS AN *AMAZING* FIRST MATCH!
NOT ONLY THAT, THEY'RE FIGHTING *SO* FAST...
...I CAN BARELY KEEP UP JUST *DESCRIBING* IT!

OMIGOSH! THIS IS SOOOOO INCREDIBLE!
WOW! LOOKS MORE LIKE THE *FINALS* THAN THE FIRST ROUND OF THE TOURNAMENT!
ZZAP
DMM
WHAM
MO

AAGH!
KA-BLAM

OOPS! SORRY 'BOUT THAT.
GRIN
MAYBE EVERYONE SHOULD BACK UP A BIT... THIS MIGHT GET A LITTLE BIT DANGEROUS. ♡

HWOOOO
WHEEZE

HEY! THE GOOD SEATS ARE EMPTY NOW!
RUSSHH

WHAT UNPRECEDENTED MANNERS ON THE PART OF THE CHAMPION!
YAAAH!
SPECTATORS, PLEASE STEP BACK!

HARETA!
LEAP
WE CAN GET A CLOSER LOOK!
THUD
THIS IS GREAT!
WAIT A MINUTE... WHO'S THAT?

YOU HAD TO GET A CLOSER LOOK TOO, HUH? PRETTY EXCITING, ISN'T IT?

HEY!

IS THIS YOUR POKÉMON?

OW!

KEEP YOUR HANDS OFF OTHER PEOPLE'S POKÉMON!

HEY, YOU!
THAT WAS KINDA RUDE, DON'TCHA THINK?
?!
HEY! WHAT ARE YOU DOING?!

A TRAINER HAS TO TAKE SPECIAL CARE OF HIS POKÉMON BEFORE A MATCH.
HE'S THE ONE WHO STEPPED OUT OF LINE BY TRYING TO TOUCH ANOTHER TRAINER'S POKÉMON!

NEVER MIND. YOU'RE RIGHT. TOTALLY HIS FAULT!
DUMMY!

STILL, YOU DIDN'T HAVE TO...
SNEAK SNEAK

HEY!

LET'S HAVE A BATTLE!

WATCHING THAT AMAZING BATTLE IN THE RING HAS GOT ME RARING TO GO!
LET'S DO IT!

PLUS, YOU'RE STRONG, AREN'T YOU? I CAN TELL.
YOU HAVE A VIBE EXACTLY LIKE THE OTHER STRONG TRAINERS I'VE MET!

BOOM
TEP
INFER-NAPE, FOCUS BLAST!
DWOOM
VWAAH
DODGE IT, GAR-CHOMP!

OH NO...
LOOK OUT!
FWOOOOSH
DA-WOOOSH
HWOOOOO

DOOM

THAT'S METAGROSS! AND THEY *EASILY* BLOCKED THAT ATTACK!
I *KNEW* IT! YOU *ARE* REALLY STRONG!
WE'RE GONNA FIGHT LATER FOR SURE!

THIS POKÉMON BATTLE IS ON!
!
SLICK, SHARP-EYED... THIS ONE LOOKS LIKE SOMETHING SPECIAL.
I BETTER TEST HIM...

GOOD! THEY'RE SAFE!

HUH ...?

HARETA ?!

BUT WHO'S *THAT* KID!

HEY, MITSUMI! EYES FRONT! YOU'RE FIGHTING *ME*, REMEMBER?

I GIVE UP.
YOU WIN THE BATTLE, CYNTHIA!
WHA—?!
WHY, W-WOULD YOU...?
TP TP TP
OH. Y'SEE...
I THINK...
...IT'S GONNA BE **MORE** FUN **WATCHING** THE TOURNAMENT THAN **FIGHTING** IN IT!

THAT LOOK IN YOUR EYES!
I GUESS YOU'RE UP FOR IT, HUH?

LET'S GO, EMPO...

... LEON ...?!

WHSH

WHAM

BAM

?!

EMPOLEON?!

DOOM

THAT'S SUCKER PUNCH! AN ATTACK WHERE...

...YOU READ YOUR OPPONENT'S MOVES AND STRIKE *BEFORE* HE DOES! THAT KID'S USING ABSOL'S SKILLS REALLY WELL...

HARETA'S RIGHT... HE *IS* A REALLY STRONG TRAINER!

EMPOLEON HAS A SERIOUS INJURY FROM ABSOL'S SPECIAL ABILITY... SUPER LUCK.
HE PROBABLY NEEDS TO HEAL.

PSHHH
THAT ONE ATTACK TOLD ME *EVERYTHING* I NEED TO KNOW.
YOU'RE NOT *WORTH* BATTLING.
SPIN

I HAVE A SIXTH SENSE FOR SNIFFING OUT *MEDIOCRE* TRAINERS.
I WONDER WHY HARETA GOT ME ALL RILED UP THEN...?

HUH? WHAT IS IT, ABSOL? WHAT DO YOU SENSE?

PING

CRACK

BOOM

WHAT'S G-GOING ON?!

HUH?!

THAT WAS A GOOD FIRST SHOT, BUT DON'T GO AWAY YET!

THIS BATTLE'S JUST GETTING STARTED!
SPLOOSH
SPLASH
SPLISH
GET READY, ABSOL!
CLENCH
HERE WE GO! SUPER SURF, EMPOLEON!
SPLOOOOSH

YOI-NK
HUH ...?
I-IT'S FROZEN!
KLINKINKINK

MITSUMI!

THAT'S GLACEON'S ICE BEAM.

DUMMY!

WHAT'RE YOU THINKING, BATTLING HERE...AND NOW?!

WHY ***NOT?*** THIS ***IS*** A POKÉMON TOURNAMENT, RIGHT? WE'RE ***SUPPOSED*** TO BATTLE!

NOT IN THE ***STANDS!***

I KNEW IT! YOU JUST DON'T GET IT!

LISTEN, HARETA DOESN'T KNOW WHAT HE'S DOING... SO COULD YOU PLEASE GIVE HIM A BREAK?

HEY! WAIT! WHAT'S YOUR NAME?!

I'M KOYA.

I'LL BE WAITING FOR YOU IN A REAL TOURNAMENT BATTLE.

I KNEW IT!

THIS CHAMPION-SHIP IS GOING TO GET *REALLY* INTERESTING!

SHEESH! FOR AN ELITE TRAINER, HE SURE IS A *JERK!*

NO WAY AM I GONNA LOSE TO *HIM!*

BUT *I'M* THE ONE WHO'S GOING TO WIN!

YOU DON'T LIKE HIM? I THOUGHT HE WAS A LOT OF FUN!

HUH?!

RIGHT HERE, TODAY!

I'M GONNA BECOME THE ***NUMBER ONE*** TRAINER!

THIS TIME...
I HAD A BIG PART! ♡

CHAPTER 2
HARETA'S HEART'S DESIRE

SINNOH TOURNAMENT STANDARD RULES

- Competition in single battles only.
- Contestants may register up to six Pokémon. Only three of those may be used in any single battle.
- Contestants may change their six registered Pokémon between battles.

ANOTHER BATTLE RAGES ON IN THIS YEAR'S SINNOH TOURNAMENT! ALTHOUGH THE TOURNAMENT IS ONLY FOR...
...EXCEPTIONAL TRAINERS, SUCH AN INCREDIBLY HIGH LEVEL OF COMPETITION IS UNHEARD OF!
PANT
GASP
TODAY'S EXCITING MATCH PITS JUN AGAINST KOYA...

USING ABSOL, KOYA HAS DEFEATED BOTH TORTERRA AND STARAPTOR WITH SINGLE STRIKES! AND NOW JUN IS DOWN TO HIS LAST POKÉMON!
KOYA IS ONE OF THE MOST SKILLED TRAINERS TO ARRIVE ON THE SCENE IN QUITE SOME TIME!

IT'S NOT THAT JUN IS WEAK...

...THIS NEW GUY IS JUST *TOO* STRONG!

C'MON ...

YOU CAN *DO* IT, JUN!

YOU CAN STILL BEAT THIS GUY!

YEAH! YOU'RE RIGHT!

POP

I'M NOT GOING DOWN WITHOUT A FIGHT!

I'LL SHOW HIM WHAT I'M MADE OF!

DRAGONITE, GO!

POP

GWEEEEEEEEEE
HYPER BEAM!
...IRON TAIL!!
WHAK
ABSOL, DETECT!
AND...
GWEEEEE
WHAAAM

HURRRRAH
I-IT'S OVER! THE MATCH LASTED BARELY A MINUTE.
KOYA WON THE BATTLE WITH A SHOW OF OVER-WHELMING STRENGTH!
HEY...
YOU'RE **REALLY** TOUGH! I WAS TOTALLY OUT-CLASSED!
WELL, ALL I CAN DO IS LAUGH IT OFF!
GOOD LUCK IN YOUR NEXT MATCH! I'LL DEFINITELY BE WATCHING!
REACH

PEOPLE LIKE YOU HAVE ***NO RIGHT*** TO BE POKÉMON TRAINERS.

YOU HAVE NO TALENT. YOU SHOULDN'T EVEN BE ALLOWED TO HANDLE POKÉMON.
THE WAY YOU PLAY AROUND, YOU'LL END UP HURTING THEM.

TRAINERS LIKE YOU RAISE UNHAPPY POKÉMON.
...

I HAVE NOTHING ELSE TO SAY. GOODBYE.

POUNCE

HEY!

THUD

KOYA!
WHAT'S **WRONG** WITH YOU? THERE'S NO REASON TO BE SO **RUDE** TO JUN!

JUN'S POKÉMON AREN'T UNHAPPY!
SURE, HE'S A WEAK TRAINER COMPARED TO **YOU**, BUT...
OH, THANKS A LOT, HARETA. I FEEL BETTER ALREADY.

...HE **LOVES** HIS POKÉMON, AND HE TAKES **GOOD CARE** OF THEM!
AND ANOTHER THING—
WHAT-EVER. HE'S A LOSER.

...WHEN YOU'RE SUCH A NOVICE YOURSELF! HAVE YOU EVER COMPETED IN A TOURNAMENT BEFORE?
WHAT? WAIT, KOYA!
KLK KLK
BETTER NOT WASTE YOUR TIME WORRYING ABOUT OTHER TRAINERS...
ANYWAY, ISN'T YOUR BATTLE ABOUT TO START?
URK!

GRRR...

FEEL SORRY FOR ME, MITSUMI!

THE NEXT BATTLE IS ABOUT TO BEGIN!

GOOD LUCK, HARETA.

DARN THAT KOYA! I WANT TO TELL HIM WHAT I THINK ABOUT POKÉMON AND BATTLES, BUT...

...HE GETS ME SO ***FLUSTERED*** IT DOESN'T COME OUT RIGHT!

KOYA'S ***WRONG!*** BUT I'LL HAVE TO...

...***BATTLE*** HIM TO ***SHOW*** HIM!

SO I'VE ***GOTTA*** KEEP WINNING UNTIL I FACE KOYA!
THEN HE'LL ***SEE*** THE TRUTH! OH YES, HE WILL!
DOOOM
WOW! HARETA IS REALLY PUMPED!

AND HIS OPPONENT IS ONLY JUST NOW ENTERING THE STADIUM!

?
VROOM
VROOOM

BOOM
BOOM
BOOM

BUDDA BOOM BOOM
BOOM
SORRY TO KEEP YOU WAITING, HARETA!
I'M FLINT! ONE OF THE SINNOH ELITE FOUR!
FLASH
W-WHAT THE ...?!
LEAP
HA HA!
TUP

WINK
I CAME TO THIS COMPETITION BECAUSE I HEARD ABOUT YOUR REP.
I'M EXPECTING *YOU* TO GIVE ME A HEART-POUNDING, INTENSE POKÉMON BATTLE!

HEY! AWESOME ENTRANCE! WHAT A JUMP!
IF YOU THINK *THAT* WAS SOMETHING...
...PREPARE TO BE *DAZZLED* BY MY BATTLE SKILLS, HARETA!

ALL RIGHT! LET'S DO IT!
OH YEEAAAH! GOOD ANSWER!
YOU'RE PRETTY GROOVY FOR A LITTLE DUDE, SO...

...BEFORE WE BATTLE— LET'S *DANCE!*
BOOM BUDDA
BOOM
WHOA! I GUESS IT'S DISCO TIME!
BOOOM
BUDDA

THIS IS HIS FIRST TOURNAMENT MATCH...
WHY DOES HE HAVE TO ACT LIKE AN IDIOT?!
BOOM BOOM BUDDA BOOM

WELL, IT APPEARS THE DANCING IS OVER, SO PREPARE YOURSELF FOR...
POSE
...A POKÉMON BATTLE!

OKAY! LET'S GO, EMPOLEON!
BURN HOT! RAPIDASH!!
SINCE THAT ONE'S A FIRE-TYPE...
...WE'LL USE MY FAVORITE—HYDRO PUMP!
SPLOOSH
SORRY, HARETA!
WE'RE NOT MAKING IT *THAT* EASY!

RAPIDASH—
AGILITY!

SHWOOSH

SLOSH

OF
COURSE! I
WOULDN'T
SEND A
FIRE-TYPE
AGAINST A
WATER-
TYPE IF I
COULDN'T!

Ha Ha Ha Ha!
YA GOTTA ADMIT, THE CROWD LOVES ME!
...UNDER THE BLAZING SUN, IT'S RODEO TIME ON RAPIDASH!
BUCK
HOP
BUCK
HEY! NO FAIR!
YEE-HAW
SNAP
BUT THIS IS NO TIME TO BE HORSING AROUND!
GO FOR IT, RAPIDASH!
I WANNA RIDE TOO!
YIPPEE!
TOSS
WAGH?!
GROOVY!
THUD

SOLARBEAM BOOSTED BY SUNNY DAY!

CRACKLE

KA-BOOOM

HE'S GOOD! FLINT ***DESERVES*** TO BE IN THE ELITE FOUR!

I THOUGHT YOU MIGHT APPRECIATE THAT TECHNIQUE.

SUNNY DAY CUTS DOWN ON THE CHARGE TIME FOR SOLAR-BEAM.

THUD

TOSS
LET'S GO!!

UGH... I WALKED RIGHT INTO THAT ONE!
OKAY! TIME TO GET SERIOUS!

WHAM!

OOOOO!

AH, NOW *THAT'S* AN IMPRESSIVE POKÉMON!

WHOA!

REGIGIGAS, HUH? I'VE HEARD OF IT!

IT'S GOT SLOW START! IT WON'T BE ABLE TO MOVE FOR A WHILE!

YEAH, EXCEPT...

I TAUGHT SKILL SWAP TO MISDREAVUS...

...AND I'M GONNA *SWITCH* THEIR POWERS!

POP

...YOU CAN ONLY HAVE ONE POKÉMON ON THE FIELD AT A TIME!
HOLD IT! THAT'S AGAINST THE RULES! IN TOURNAMENTS...
TWEET
HUH? SERIOUSLY?
TWEEET
PWEET
TWEEET
ANOTHER VIOLATION! TRAINERS ARE NOT ALLOWED TO FIGHT!
WHAA-?
TWEEET
WELL THEN...
BUMP
I GUESS I'LL HAVE TO JOIN THE FIGHT MYSELF!
OH, I GET IT... HARETA'S A TOTAL BEGINNER!
THEN THIS BATTLE IS OVER.
I GUESS THIS MATCH WON'T BE FUN AFTER ALL, HARETA.
SO I'LL JUST FINISH THIS OFF QUICK!

IF YOU WANNA SURRENDER, NOW'S THE TIME!
MISDREA-VUS!

IT'S LIKE KOYA SAID... IF YOU DON'T HAVE THE SKILL, YOU'LL END UP ***HURTING*** YOUR POKÉMON.

YOU CAN'T PROTECT YOUR POKÉMON WITH YOUR BODY.

TOURNAMENTS ARE BATTLES WITH STRICT ***RULES.***

I CAN'T USE SKILL SWAP...
IF THIS KEEPS UP, MISDREA-VUS WILL GET...

THE WAY YOU PLAY AROUND, YOU'LL END UP HURTING THEM.

PEOPLE LIKE YOU HAVE ***NO RIGHT*** TO BE POKÉMON TRAINERS.

YOU SHOULDN'T EVEN BE ALLOWED TO ***HANDLE*** POKÉMON.

W-WHAT THE—?!

THAT'S NOT TRUE!

ROAR

...

CLENCH

TH...

KOYA!
YOU BETTER BE WATCHING THIS MATCH!

WHAT ...?
HE'S NOT EVEN *LOOKING* AT ME?!
DON'T UNDER-ESTIMATE ME!

DRIFBLIM! PAYBACK!
VWAH
DREE!
MISDREAVUS! SKILL SWAP!
PING

FLASH
KABLOOOE
W-WHAT IN THE WORLD ...?!
MISDREAVUS... EXPLODED ?!
WHAM
I GET IT! THAT'S DRIFBLIM'S SPECIALTY... AFTERMATH!
INSTEAD OF USING SKILL SWAP ON REGIGIGAS, HE USED IT ON US!
WE'RE NOT DONE YET!
I'LL BLAST YOU WITH SOLAR BEAM AGAIN!
BRING IT ON!

DOOM

REGIGIGAS, GO!

I'LL GET YOU WHILE IT'S STILL IN SLOW-START MODE!

FRY THEM WITH SOLAR BEAM!

DWEEEEEE
HOLD ON, REGIGIGAS!

DWEEEEEE
YOU CAN DO IT, REGIGIGAS...
HA! IT CAN'T POSSIBLY HOLD ON!
KRK

BECAUSE POKÉMON CARE ABOUT THEIR TRAINERS...
THEY *LOVE* US!
IT'S MY FAULT YOU GOT HURT TODAY—EMPOLEON AND MISDREAVUS TOO...
...BUT *NONE* OF YOU IS UNHAPPY!

AND I LOVE THEM ALL TOO! THAT'S WHY...
I HAVE TO FIGHT AS HARD AS THEY DO!
REGIGIGAS!
?!
VOOOM
I-IT'S MOVING?!

WHABAM

YOU HAD ME GOING THERE FOR A SECOND! IT *HAD* TO MOVE...
...SO IT COULD *FALL DOWN!*
HEH...
HEH HEH...

YOU KEEP TRYING, AND ONE DAY SOON...
HUH?
LOOM
YOU NEW TRAINERS ARE SOMETHING SPECIAL.
DON'T LET LOSSES LIKE THIS GET YOU DOWN.
Y'KNOW WHAT, HARETA? YOU DID GOOD.
YOU GOT MY HEART RACING.

WHAAA ?!
WHAT A SOUND!
REGIGIGAS HAS *AWAKENED* AT LAST!
RRRROOOOOOOAR
ALL RIGHT, REGIGIGAS!
BUST OUT THAT MOVE YOU'VE BEEN HOLDING BACK ALL THIS TIME!

ROARING
MEGA PUNCH!

GLEAM
SO THAT'S THE POWER OF REGIGIGAS!
SHING
W-WHAT AWESOME POWER!
EVEN THOUGH REGIGIGAS IS HURT AND EXHAUSTED... THEIR TRUST IS UNBREAKABLE!
WOW! THAT'S KINDA DEEP!
COME ON, FLINT! LET'S SEE YOUR NEXT POKÉMON...
NOPE. I'M NOT BRINGING IT OUT.
HUH?
SWSH
STEELIX IS MY LAST ONE, AND IT CAN'T WIN AGAINST REGIGIGAS.
I HAD A LOT OF FUN.
I'M LOOKING FORWARD TO YOUR NEXT BATTLES—AS A SPECTATOR!

YOU WIN, HARETA!
YOUR RAPPORT WITH YOUR POKÉMON IS IMPRESSIVE!
HURRAAAYYYY
IT'S A TRIUMPH FOR OUR UNDERDOG CONTESTANT! CONGRATULA-TIONS!
YAAAYY
KOYA!

MY POKÉMON AND I DESERVE TO FIGHT TOGETHER BECAUSE WE REALLY LOVE EACH OTHER!
THAT'S WHAT I WANTED YOU TO UNDER-STAND!
GOT IT?!
HMPH!
YOU JUST WAIT, KOYA!
I'M GONNA BEAT YOU!

YO!

AND WITH REGIGIGAS'S SUPER POWERFUL MEGA PUNCH...
CHAPTER 3
CLASH! HARETA VS. KOYA

...HARETA CLEARS THE FIRST ROUND WITH AN UNEXPECTED WIN!
YOU JUST WAIT, KOYA!
I'M GONNA BEAT YOU!

CHEEEER
SO HARETA MANAGED TO POST A WIN IN THE SINNOH TOURNAMENT?
LIKE FATHER, LIKE SON, I GUESS.
COME TO THINK OF IT... HARETA'S FATHER WAS A FREE SPIRIT TOO!
YOU'RE GOING TO LEAVE YOUR CHILD WITH ME SO THAT YOU CAN TRAVEL?!
WHAT ARE YOU *THINKING* ?!
BAD!
YOU'LL BE A GREAT PARENT, PROFESSOR!

THERE ARE STILL *SO MANY* POKÉMON IN THE WORLD *WAITING* TO BE DISCOVERED!

MY TRAVELS MAY *NEVER* END!

THAT'S HOW IT'S GONNA BE. THANKS, PROF!
STILL CAN'T BELIEVE IT...
HOW-EVER...
SOME-HOW THINGS TURNED OUT ALL RIGHT.
HO HO HO

HEY!

GRAMPS!
BOUND
YOU'RE LOOKING GOOD, HARETA!

SQUEE!
YOU MADE IT, PROFESSOR!
YES. I WANTED TO SEE YOU IN ACTION.

GREAT! I'LL SHOW YOU ***LOTS*** OF ACTION!

CHEEEER
WE NOW RETURN TO THE SINNOH TOURNAMENT! THE FIGHTING IS...
...INCREDIBLE! YOU CAN'T AFFORD TO LOOK AWAY FOR A SECOND!

WA
PPITA
WAP
METAGROSS, METEOR MASH.

THUD
AMBIPOM!

AMBIPOM, FURY SWIPE!
LEAP
KLANG
IRON DEFENSE.
WHY ...?
WHY ...?
WHY ISN'T EVEN ONE ATTACK GETTING THROUGH?!
HE'S AN AMAZING TRAINER.
HIS TACTICS ARE COOLY CALCULATED, AND HE READS HIS OPPONENT'S MOVES TWO OR THREE STEPS AHEAD.
YUP.

BOOOM
HAMMER ARM.
HE KNOWS ALL HIS POKÉMON'S ABILITIES...
HIS TECHNIQUE IS *PERFECT.*
HIS BATTLES ARE PRACTICALLY ROBOTICALLY SYNCHRONIZED!

STOMP
TO BEAT KOYA, HARETA WILL HAVE TO HONE HIS STRENGTHS AND SMOOTH OUT HIS ROUGH EDGES.
TO BE HONEST, I DON'T THIN HARETA'S READY FOR HIM YET.
LET'S GO! THIS IS MY CHANCE TO SHOW THE CROWD EVERYTHING I'VE GOT!
CHEEEER
BUT HARETA HAS A LOT OF POTENTIAL...
AT LEAST HE'LL GROW *A LOT* DURING THIS TOURNAMENT!

ZZZZZZ
SIGH. AT LEAST HE'S GETTING HIS BEAUTY REST.
BOOM
Ha Ha Ha
OOPS! LOOKS LIKE THE HYPNOSIS EFFECT GOT NOT ONLY MISDREAVUS BUT HARETA AS WELL!
ZZZZZ
YAWN
OH... HEY... I FELL ASLEEP FOR A SEC THERE, BUT...
...NOW I'M *RESTED* AND READY TO GO!
ROAR

SLAM
ZZZZARK
CHARGE!
HANG IN THERE, LUXIO!

WHAM
LUXIO!
HIS LUXIO LACKS SKILL. PLUS, IT'S EXHAUSTED.
THUD
CONTINUING THE BATTLE WILL ONLY HURT THAT POKÉMON.
THIS ISN'T WORTH WATCHING...

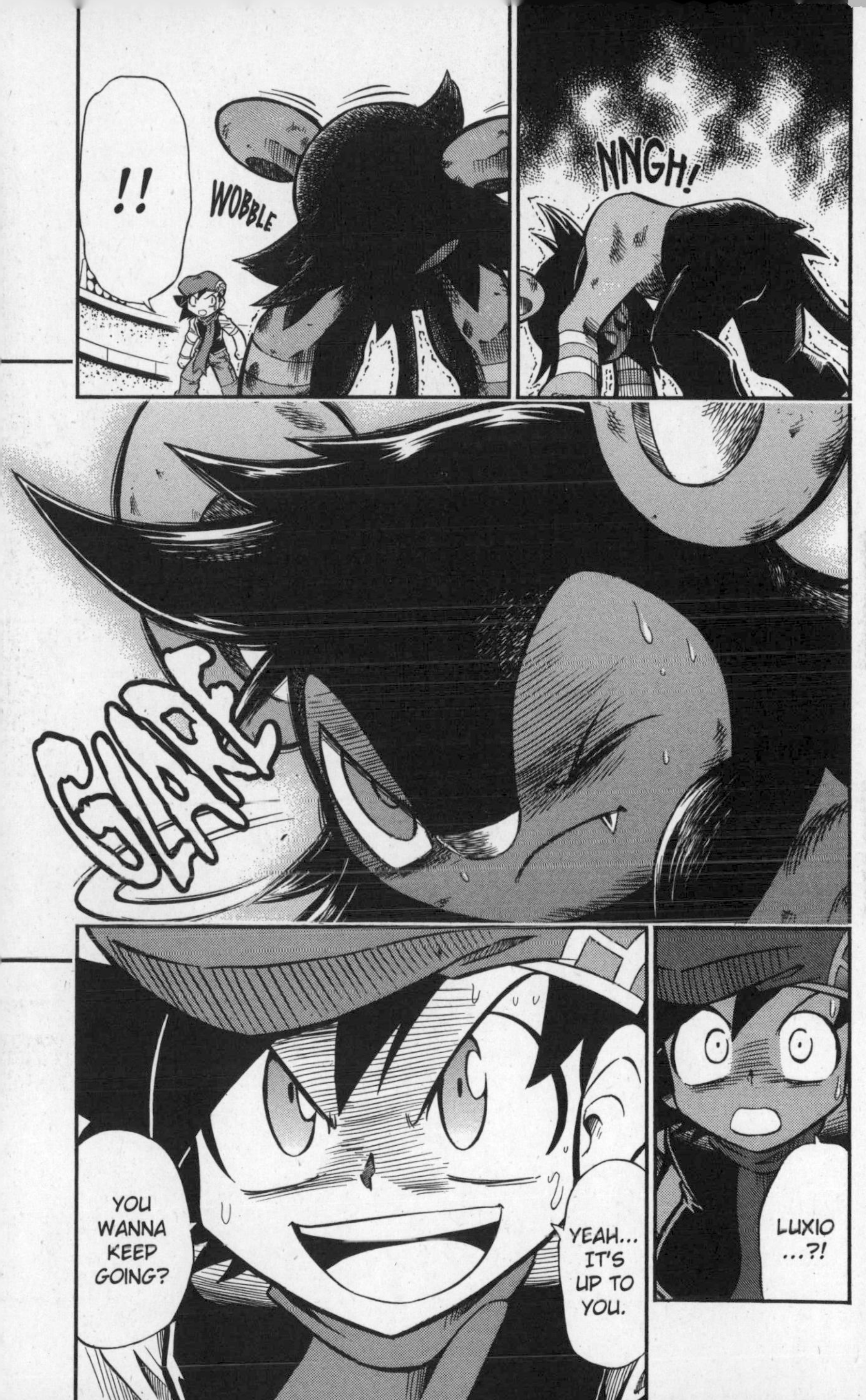

NNGH!
WOBBLE
!!
YEAH... IT'S UP TO YOU.
YOU WANNA KEEP GOING?
LUXIO ...?!

DASH
HOLD ON! HERACROSS IS LOOKING TO FINISH THIS WITH TAKE DOWN!
NOW!
DOUBLE-STRENGTH THUNDER!
KRA-KA-BOOM
FLASH

THUNK

LOOK OUT, KOYA!
I'M UP AGAINST *YOU* NEXT!

ONCE AGAIN, HARETA COMES FROM BEHIND AND WINS!
CHEEEER
HE'S MOVING ON TO THE SEMIFINALS!

HMM...
LOOKS LIKE HE MANAGED TO SCRATCH OUT ANOTHER WIN, EH, MITSUMI?
HM?
WHERE'D MITSUMI GO?

YES.
WITHOUT A DOUBT.
YES, WITH PROFESSOR ROWAN.
YES...
I'LL GO ON WITH MY MISSION.
CLAMP
SPIN

AND WHAT WAS *THAT* ALL ABOUT?

WHAT COULD BE MORE IMPORTANT THAN SEEING WHO YOUR NEXT OPPONENT WILL BE?

EAVES-DROPPING? YOU'RE A VERY RUDE GIRL.

MAYBE. BUT *YOU'RE* THE ONE WHO *STARTED* THE EAVES-DROPPING.
TUP
OR DIDN'T YOU THINK ANYONE NOTICED YOU BACK THERE...?

KOYA?

THE A-BLOCK SEMIFINAL MATCH WILL BEGIN SHORTLY.

PLAYERS, PLEASE MAKE YOUR WAY TO THE STADIUM.

SPIN

YOU *THINK* YOU'VE GOT ME FIGURED OUT, DON'T YOU? LET ME ASSURE YOU...

...IF YOU GET IN MY WAY...

...YOU *WILL* BE ELIMINATED.

GOODBYE.

TEP TEP TEP

CREEP!

AND NOW...WHAT YOU'VE ALL BEEN WAITING FOR...THE FIRST SEMIFINAL MATCH!
HURRRAAYY
GRIND
CRUNCH
WAAH

HARD TO BELIEVE YOU MADE IT THIS FAR...

...BUT YOUR LUCK RUNS OUT *NOW!*

POP

ONLY A CHOSEN FEW CAN BECOME TRAINERS.

AND YOU HAVEN'T EARNED THAT RIGHT.

CLUTCH

I DON'T *CARE* ABOUT RIGHT... OR LEFT!

BECAUSE OUR BATTLE'S GONNA BE *AMAZING!*

GRIN

I'M JUST REALLY *HAPPY* RIGHT NOW!

POP

ARE YOU READY TO BRING IT ON, KOYA?

CHEEER
...SEMIFINAL POKÉMON BATTLE...
AND NOW, LET THE SINNOH TOURNAMENT ...
...BEGIN!
DASH
YOU'RE ABOUT TO LEARN HOW DIFFERENT OUR SKILL LEVELS ARE!
LET'S GO!
YEAH! LET'S DO THIS!

SWSH
CRACKLE
LUXIO, THUN—
VWSH
?!
SUCKER PUNCH!
SMACK

WHAM
LUXIO!

I OBSERVED YOUR LUXIO'S ABILITIES IN ITS LAST BATTLE.
IT'S NO COMPETITION FOR ABSOL. YOU MIGHT AS WELL GIVE UP NOW!

HE'S STRONG!
YEAH. AND HE WANTS TO COMPLETELY CRUSH HARETA.
CONSIDERING KOYA'S FLAWLESS BATTLE TACTICS...
I WOULDN'T GIVE HARETA EVEN A 1 PERCENT CHANCE OF WINNING.

SKIIIIIDD
HANG IN THERE, LUXIO!
STAND UP!
STOP IT!
THAT'S NO BATTLE STRATEGY! IT'S JUST POINTLESS CHEER-LEADING!
YOU MIGHT THINK IT'S USELESS...
...BUT I'M SHOWING HIM HOW I FEEL!
AND IF MY EMOTION GETS THROUGH TO HIM...
...LUXIO WILL STAND UP!

RIDICULOUS TRICKS LIKE THAT DON'T WIN BATTLES!
I'LL MAKE THAT CRYSTAL CLEAR TO YOU!
IRON TAIL!
SHACK
WOOOOoo
LUXIO!

WHAM
WOOOOOO
UNGH!
BLOOM
HARETA!

HWOOOOH
HARETA!
HARETA...

HA...
...RE...
...TA...
HARETA!

LISTEN UP, HARETA.

DON'T *EVER* NEGLECT YOUR POKÉMON. GIVE THEM ALL THE LOVE IN YOUR HEART. TREAT THEM LIKE FAMILY.

IF YOU DO, THEY WILL ***ALWAYS*** BE THERE FOR YOU.

MURMUR
MURMUR
MEDIC TO THE FIELD! HURRY!
TROT TROT TROT
I LET MYSELF GET RILED UP AGAIN.
BUT IT'S OVER NOW. THE BATTLE IS...
HUH?
FLASH
WHA- ?!
GLOW
?!

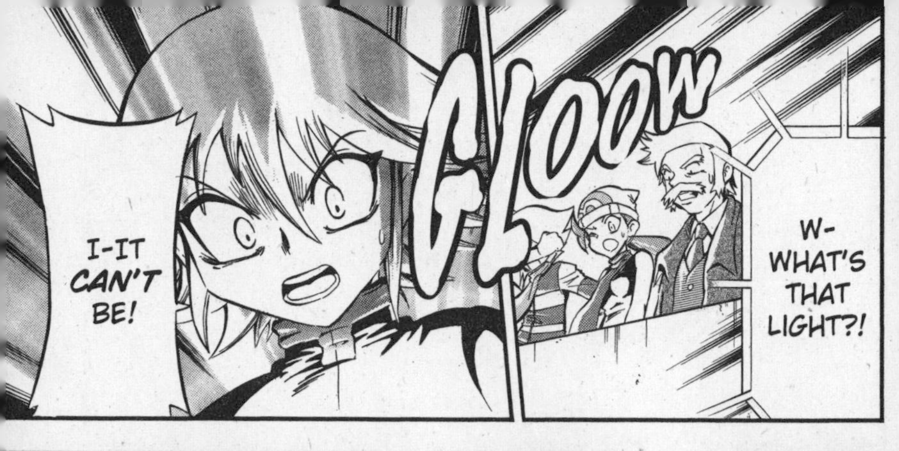

W-WHAT'S THAT LIGHT?!
GLOOW
I-IT *CAN'T* BE!

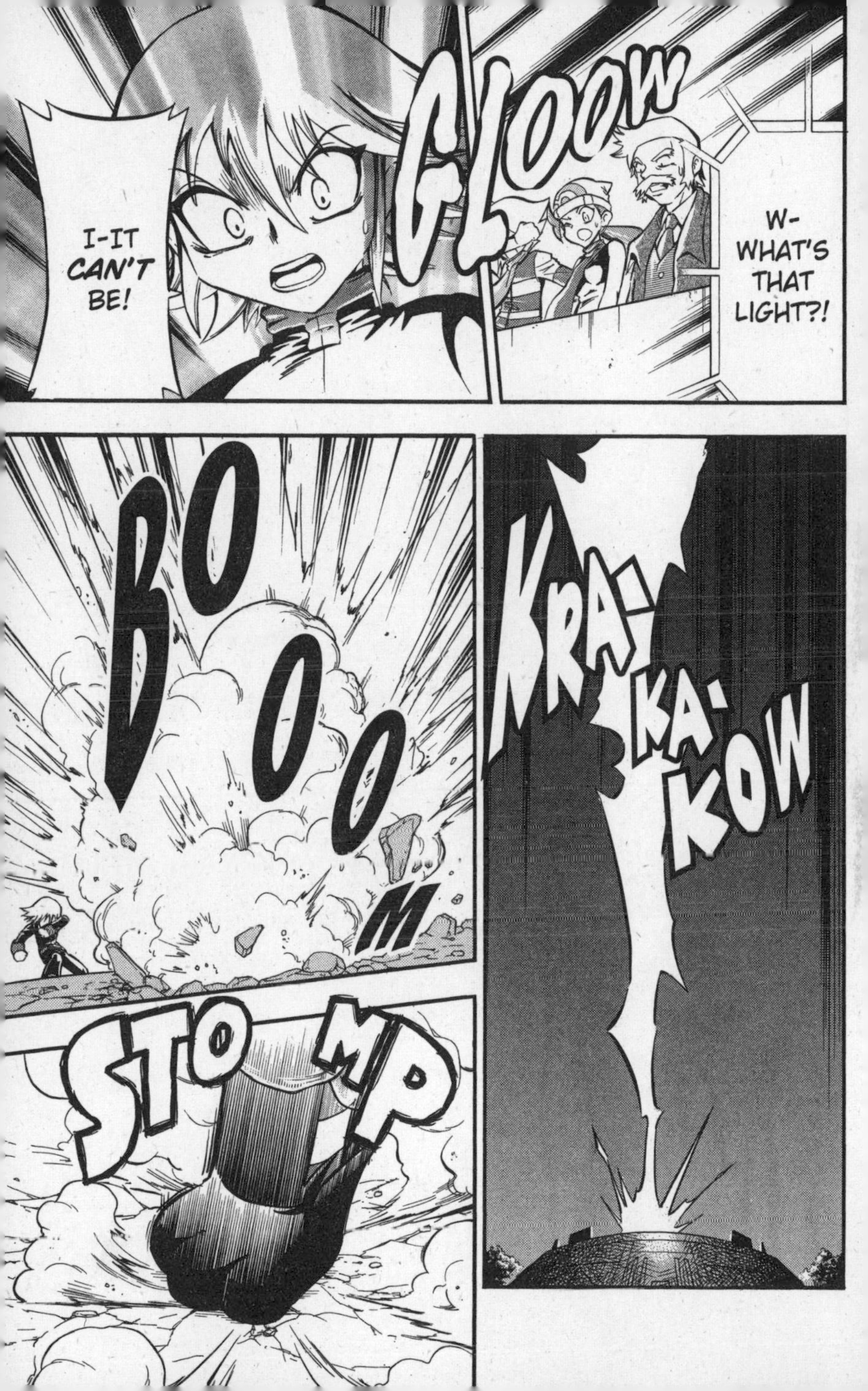

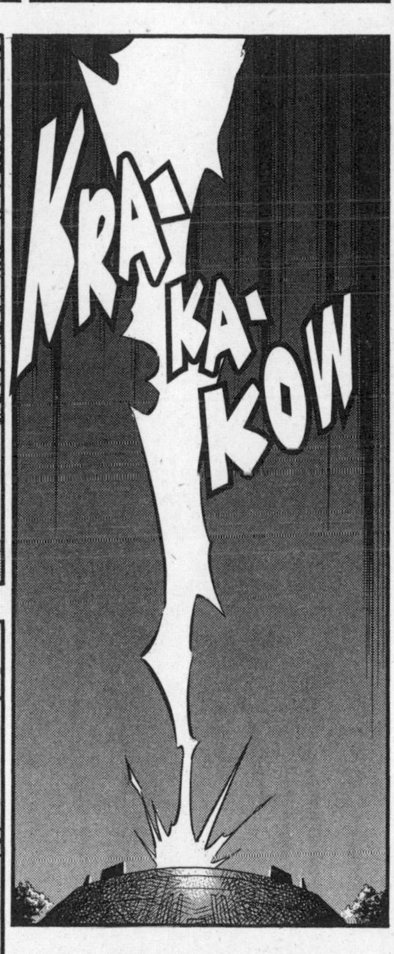

BOOOOM

STOMP

U...
UNBELIEV-ABLE!
LUXIO EVOLVED INTO LUXRAY!
HURRAH

I *SENSED* THAT LUXIO WANTED TO EVOLVE!
THAT'S WHY I LET HIM DO WHAT HE WANTED AND KEPT ON BATTLING WITH HIM!
HE KEPT LUXIO OUT BECAUSE HE *ANTICI-PATED* AN EVOLUTION?
?!
GOOD JOB, HARETA!
THAT'S YOUR STRENGTH—BEING IN TUNE WITH YOUR POKÉMON!
THAT TURNS A 1 PERCENT POSSIBILITY INTO A 100 PERCENT CERTAINTY!

IF YOU OPEN YOUR HEART TO YOUR POKÉMON, KOYA...
...THEY'LL *ALWAYS* ANSWER!
HEY, WAIT... I THINK...
HUH?
WHERE HAVE I HEARD THAT BEFORE...?
GRIN
OH WELL! WHAT-EVER.
THIS BATTLE IS JUST GETTING *STARTED!*

CHAPTER 4
HEARTS AND SPIRITS COLLIDE
AMAZING! HARETA'S LUXIO EVOLVED INTO LUXRAY!

LET'S GO, KOYA!
THIS SEMIFINAL BATTLE IS STILL UP FOR GRABS!

EVEN WITH THAT EVOLUTION, YOU STILL CAN'T WIN AGAINST ME!
I'M SWITCHING TO META-GROSS!
POP

ROAR
DO WHATEVER YOU LIKE. I *TOLD* YOU...I'M GOING TO *WIN!* GO, LUXRAY!!
BZZAP
THUNDER FANG!
GLARE
YAY!
HE GOT A BLOW IN!

METAGROSS, EARTHQUAKE!
THUD
L- LUXRAY!

HE PLANNED THAT! HE WANTED METAGROSS TO DO EARTH-QUAKE!
SO HIS STRATEGY IS TO FIGHT HARETA, NOT HIS POKÉMON?!
AMAZING! YOU'RE GOOD, KOYA!
PLOP
KEEP IT UP! READY FOR MY NEXT MOVE?
DOOOM
OH YEAH!
NOW THIS BATTLE GETS SERIOUS!
THAT'S RIGHT!
MUNCH
MUNCH

MIFF IFF WURF VA FAFFLE GEFF FEERIUFF!
(THIS IS WHERE THE FIGHT GETS SERIOUS!)

GO!

GO, HARETA!

DOGOOM
OKAY! LET'S DO THIS, REGIGIGAS!
GOOD ONE, HARETA!

PART OF IT IS FIGHTING AGAINST SOMEONE AS GOOD AS KOYA, BUT...

...THERE'S SOMETHING *ELSE*... I DON'T KNOW WHAT, BUT SOMETHING *SPECIAL* IS HAPPENING HERE!

YEAH!

THIS BATTLE IS A BLAST!

WOW! THOSE ARE SOME FIERCE ATTACKS FROM HARETA!
CHEEEEER
PERFECT!
YOU CAN DO THIS, HARETA!
KOYA!
IT'S JUST LIKE I THOUGHT! BATTLING YOU IS BEYOND COOL!
IT'S AWESOME FUN!
...
"FUN" ...?
PLOP

CLA
TT
DOOM
MAMO-
SWINE!

?!
TH-THAT'S MAMOSWINE !?
RUMMMMMMBLE
KICK THEM AWAY, MAMO-SWINE!
TAKE DOWN!
SLAM

BOOM

WHAM

WHAT INCREDIBLE POWER! IT TOOK DOWN REGIGIGAS WITH *ONE* BLOW!

PANT
GASP

YOU TALK ABOUT *HAVING FUN...*
HUFF
PUFF

THERE'S NO ROOM FOR POINTLESS FEELINGS LIKE THAT IN BATTLE!
ONCE I TOO WAS...
...A TRAINER WHO HAD FUN DURING MY BATTLES.
MY FIRST POKÉMON WAS GROWLITHE.
EEK!
WE ALWAYS BATTLED TOGETHER.
IT WASN'T ABOUT WINNING OR LOSING.
WE FOUGHT FOR THE SHEER JOY OF IT!
BUT...
DWOOSH

ONE DAY WE EXPERIENCED A CRUSHING DEFEAT.
I FOOLISHLY CHALLENGED AN OPPONENT WHO WAS TOO STRONG!
I'M SORRY, GROWLITHE!
PHYSICALLY, IT'S FINE.
UNFORTUNATELY...
HIYA, GROWLITHE...
SHIVER
...

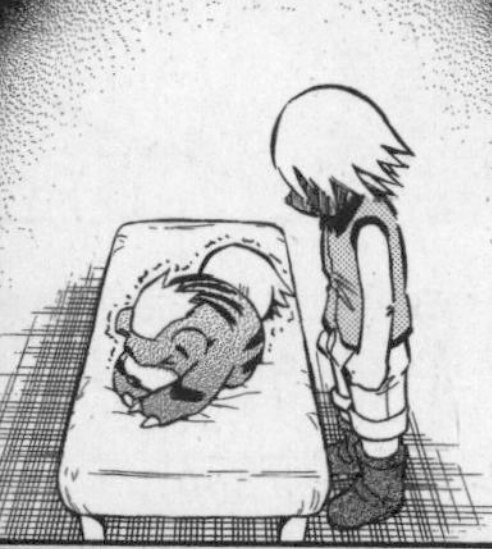
THAT BATTLE BROKE MY GROWLITHE'S SPIRIT.
MY BRAVE GROWLITHE WAS NO MORE...

IF I'D HAD A PROPER BATTLE PLAN, GROWLITHE WOULDN'T HAVE GOTTEN CRUSHED!

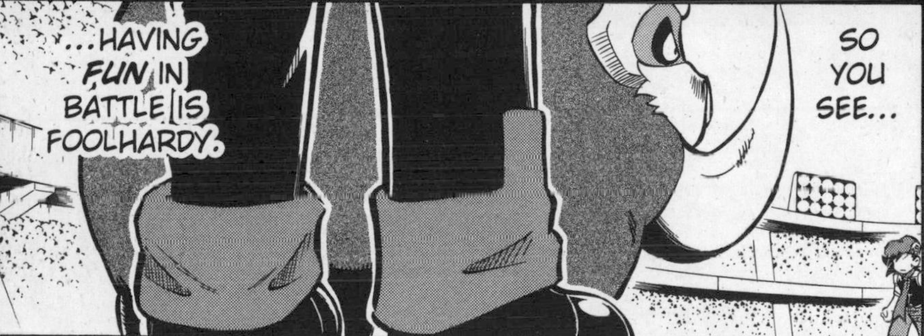
SO YOU SEE...
...HAVING FUN IN BATTLE IS FOOLHARDY.

A PERFECT WIN...
...THAT IS A POKEMON TRAINER'S DUTY!

SWH
KOYA'S LOOKING A LITTLE SCARY...
UM...
ROOOAAR
HAIL!
MAMO-SWINE!
GLARE

HWOOSH
AAH!
HWOOOOSH
IT'S COMING DOWN HARD!
WAH!
HWOOOOOOOOOSH
OUT OF NOWHERE, HAIL IS POURING FROM THE SKY!
HWOOOOOOOOO
HAVING FUN IS INAPPROPRIATE DURING A BATTLE!
AND YOU ARE UNACCEPTABLE AS A TRAINER!

I DON'T KNOW WHY YOU'RE SUCH A SOURPUSS, KOYA, BUT I'M NOT GONNA JUST TAKE WHATEVER YOU DISH OUT!
POP
EMPOLEON, HYDRO PUMP!
SPLOOSH
HWOOOOOOOO
?!
FWOOSH
I-IT MISSED?!

MAMOSWINE, TAKE DOWN!

PAM

WAIT! MAMOSWINE *DISAP-PEARED?!*

WHERE'D IT GO?!

FWSH

?!

THAT'S MAMO-SWINE'S SNOW CLOAK.
USING THAT AS *CAMOU-FLAGE,* IT CAN *SNEAK UP* ON ITS OPPONENTS.
THAT'S ANOTHER TACTIC GEARED JUST FOR HARETA!
EMPOLEON!

A COLD AND CALCULATED BATTLE STRATEGY...

...CREATED TO *CRUSH* HARETA!

KEEP IT UP, EMPOLEON! ONE MORE BLAST!

SPLOOSH

SLOOSH

IT'S NO USE...

POW

MAMO-SWINE, TAKE DOWN!

HARETA! TAKE DOWN DOESN'T HURT EMPOLEON MUCH, BUT GETTING HIT BY SO *MANY* IS ADDING UP!

WITH ALL THIS HAIL IT'S HARD TO...

HWOOOO OO

IT'S NO USE. YOU SHOULD JUST GIVE UP.

LOOK. EMPOLEON'S BEATEN DOWN.
THIS IS THE RESULT OF YOUR "FUN"!

WITH THE CHILDISH NOTION THAT BATTLES ARE FUN...
...YOU'LL **NEVER** DEFEAT ME!
HWOOOOOOO
GRRR...

WHAT'S WRONG? WHY ARE YOU SILENT?
YOU DON'T AGREE WITH HIM, DO YOU?!
HE MIGHT HAVE BETTER SKILLS THAN YOU, BUT YOU'VE GOT MORE *SPIRIT!*
USE YOUR SPIRIT—AND YOUR EMOTION! FIGHT WITH *THEM!!*
YOUR POKÉMON WILL RESPOND TO YOUR PASSION!

W-WHAT THE ...?

TH-THAT VOICE!
IT C-CAN'T BE...!

SPIN
GRIN
YEAH! THAT'S RIGHT! I'M *NOT* GONNA LET HIM BEAT US!
AND WE'RE GONNA KEEP HAVING *FUN!*
RAH

WE'RE GOING TO HAVE LOTS AND LOTS OF FUN, RIGHT, EMPOLEON?!
GRIN
I SEE...
THEN I'LL JUST HAVE TO *BEAT* THIS NONSENSE OUT OF YOU!
CHARGE
EMPOLEON CAN'T HANDLE ANOTHER TAKE DOWN!
HARETA!

FWUMP

WHAT ...?!

WHAT ARE YOU D-DOING? THIS IS NO TIME TO FALL DOWN!
FUME
GET UP, HARETA!

IGNORE HIM, MAMO-SWINE!

EMPOLEON CAN'T SEE YOU ANYWAY!

RUMMMMBLE

HARETA, GET UP!

THAT VIBRATION ...

...IT'S GETTING CLOSER.

RUMBLE

MAMO-SWINE'S TAKE DOWN...

...I **SEE** IT!

JERK
EMPOLEON!
VWIP
MOVE RIGHT!
MAMO?!
THEY CAUGHT US?!
HE LAY ON THE GROUND TO TRACK MAMOSWINE'S FOOTSTEPS!

GO!

RAGING
RAPIDS
HYDRO
PUMP!!

GOOM
HYDRO PUMP DID IT!
CHEEEER
HARETA MANAGED THAT CRISIS MAGNIFI-CENTLY!
GLEAM

THAT'S THE STUFF, HARETA! GOOD JOB!
USE YOUR INTENSITY!
ATTABOY! THAT'S MY SON!
ZOOM

THAT MAN OVER THERE. HIS NAME IS KAISEI...

HUH? WHO?!

I-IT REALLY *IS* HIM!

...AND HE'S HARETA'S *FATHER!*
WHAAAAT?!

WOW!
I CAN SEE THE RESEMBLANCE... SORTA.

THAT'S RIGHT, THAT'S THE BOY'S FATHER.
INFILTRATING THIS TOURNAMENT TURNED OUT TO BE A GREAT IDEA. HEH HEH.
STEP

MUNCH
CRUNCH
MUNCH
THIS WHITE-HOT SEMIFINAL MATCH IS ABOUT TO BE DECIDED!
IT'S TIME FOR AGENT HANSOM OF THE INTERNATIONAL POLICE TO GO INTO ACTION!
BOTH TRAINERS HAVE JUST A SINGLE POKÉMON LEFT!

WE'VE FINALLY TRACKED DOWN...
...KAISEI...

...AND HE'S THAT KID'S FATHER!
CHAPTER 5
A SURPRISE VISIT FROM HARETA'S FATHER!

CHEEER

EMPOLEON, YOU MUST BE EXHAUSTED AFTER THAT BATTLE WITH MAMOSWINE, BUT...
...YOU STILL...

...WANT TO KEEP GOING!
THAT'S RIGHT!

AQUA JET!
YOUR POKÉMON *RESPOND* TO YOUR FEELINGS!
ZWOOOSH
HANG TOUGH, ABSOL! CRUSH THEM!
BAM
WHACK

YOU JUST COULDN'T STAY AWAY FROM YOUR SON'S DEBUT MATCH, COULD YOU...

HA HA! THOSE TWO CERTAINLY ARE HAVING AN INTENSE BATTLE!

CHOMP
MUNCH
CRUNCH
...KAISEI?!

GOOD THING TOO—FOR ME! YOU'RE A KEY FIGURE IN MY CURRENT INVESTIGATION!
AND AGENT HANSOM ALWAYS GETS HIS...

HEY!

WHERE HAVE I SEEN THAT HAIRCUT BEFORE...?
COULD IT BE ...?!

FWIP

Agent Hansom's Top Secret Memo Pad

AH-HA!

SHWP

I *THOUGHT* SO!

FLIP
FLIP
FLIP

CLICK
I BETTER SPEED THINGS UP!

THAT'S A MEMBER OF TEAM GALACTIC!
I DIDN'T EXPECT *THEM* HERE!
BAM

HUH?

BEEP BEEP

BEEP BEEP

BEEP BEEP

NOW?!
A CALL...?

KOYA, DO YOU READ ME? KAISEI IS HERE!
AGENT HANSOM!
WE NEED TO APPREHEND HIM—ASAP!

REMEMBER YOUR DUTY, KOYA, AS AN AGENT OF THE INTERNATIONAL POLICE!

SORRY TO INTERRUPT YOUR BATTLE, BUT THE MISSION COMES FIRST!

DO YOU READ ME...?
HUH?!
RUSTLE

HE'S RIGHT! MY DUTIES AS AN INTERNATIONAL POLICE AGENT TAKE PRIORITY!
I KNOW I CAN'T LET A POKÉMON BATTLE INTERFERE WITH THAT... BUT I...
!

TEAM GALACTIC IS ON THE MOVE! WE'VE GOT TO NOTIFY THE POLICE!
BUT FIRST— I'VE GOT TO NAB KAISEI!
AGENT HANSOM!
DASH

HUH?
WHAT'S WRONG, KOYA?

HEY!

RUSTLE
RUSTLE
WHAT'S GOING ON...?

KABOOM
AGH!
BOOM
GWOOOH!

DOOM

A M-MYSTERIOUS POKÉMON HAS BURST INTO THE RING!

THIS IS UNHEARD-OF! A CLEAR VIOLATION OF...

SQUAWK BEEEEEP

H-HUH? THE MIC...?

WE... ARE...

WHO'S THAT ...?!

WE ARE NEO TEAM GALACTIC...

I REPEAT... WE ARE NEO TEAM GALACTIC!

LISTEN UP, YOU IGNORANT FOOLS! NEO TEAM GALACTIC IS GOING TO...

...TAKE OVER THE WORLD BY FORCE, LEAVING DESTRUCTION IN OUR WAKE...

"NEO TEAM GALACTIC" ...?!

WE REPEAT, WE ARE NEO TEAM GALACTIC!

CLENCH

WHY, YOU...!

RAAAGH
WE'RE IN THE MIDDLE OF SOMETHING IMPORTANT. BUTT OUT!!

WHO'S
TH-
THAT?

HUH...?
WHAT?

HEY,
KAISEI!
WHAT DO
YOU THINK
YOU'RE
DOING?
YOU
IDIOT!

THAT'S
RIGHT,
HARETA!
I'M
KAISEI!
I'M...
YOUR
DAD!
TA-DAH
K-
KAISEI
...?

GRIN

MY D-D-DAD ...?
IS IT *REALLY* YOU, DAD?!
AWESOME
IT'S *TRUE*... I'M YOUR DAD!
BAM
YOU'RE MY DAD!
BA-DAM
DAD! IT'S YOU!
YUP! YOUR DAD!
NOW WE KNOW ...
...WHY HARETA ACTS LIKE SUCH A BONE-HEAD!
LIKE FATHER, LIKE SON!

I'M YOUR DADDY ALL RIGHT—
WHOA!
KER-SPLAT

MITSUMI, JUN—WE NEED TO ***STOP*** THIS MAYHEM!

RIGHT!

YAAGH!

ROOAR

THIS IS NO TIME TO HORSE AROUND!

KOYA, YOU HANDLE THIS SITUATION. I'M GOING AFTER KAISEI!

ROGER.

DON'T WORRY, BOSS...

AFTER ALL, I AM AN AGENT OF THE INTERNATIONAL POLICE... AND I'LL ***CRUSH*** THIS NEW TEAM GALACTIC!

STOMP

FWOOSH
SLAM
SMACK
STOMP
STOP THIS NONSENSE!
GLARE
WITH CYRUS GONE, TEAM GALACTIC SHOULDN'T EVEN EXIST!
WHO HAD THE NERVE TO BRING BACK TEAM GALACTIC?!
HA HA HA... TEAM GALACTIC IS INDESTRUC-TIBLE!
WE HAVE A NEW LEADER TO CARRY ON CYRUS'S VISION!

OUR GREAT LEADER ***CHARON!*** HE'S LEADING TEAM GALACTIC TO A NEW AND ***GREATER*** DESTINY!

CH-
CHARON?!
?!

AND AS PROOF OF THE NEW TEAM GALACTIC'S POWER..
...WE OFFER A SAMPLE OF THE DESTRUCTION TO COME!
HEH HEH HEH HEH...
IS IT REALLY *HIM?*
SLUMP

WHAT ?!
A BOMB... *HERE?!*

WE'VE PLANTED A *BOMB* IN THIS STADIUM...
...AND WE'RE GOING TO BLOW THIS PLACE OFF THE FACE OF THE EARTH!

CHANGE OF PLANS! EVACUATE EVERY-ONE!
THE STADIUM'S ABOUT TO BE BLOWN UP!

A B-BOMB?!
YOU MEAN ...?

THERE'S A BOMB IN THE STADIUM! RUN, HARETA!

THIS OL' THING?

YES, *THAT* THING! HOW IN THE WORLD DID YOU FIND IT SO FAST?!

SHOCK

1:40

TICK TICK

I *HEARD* IT TICKING WHEN I PUT MY EAR TO THE GROUND TO LISTEN FOR MAMOSWINE.

IT WAS BURIED, SO I DUG IT UP WITH DIG!

GOOD WORK!

NOW, LIKE BEFORE IN CELESTIC TOWN, USE HYDRO PUMP TO BLAST IT INTO THE AIR SO IT'LL EXPLODE WITHOUT HARMING ANYTHING.

UNGH

O-OKAY!

TOSS
ALLEY-OOP!
HYDRO PUMP!
SPLOOOOSH
EMPOLEON, GO!
PUSH IT *HIGHER* INTO THE AIR, HARETA!
HEH HEH... IT'S NO USE!

IT'S THE END FOR ALL OF YOU!

THIS IS A SUPER-HIGH-POWERED BOMB! IT'S A HUNDRED TIMES MORE POWERFUL!
PUSH IT UP INTO THE AIR, AND THE WHOLE TOWN WILL CATCH FIRE!

WHAT ARE YOU TALKING ABOUT? IF IT'S *THAT* DESTRUCTIVE, YOU'RE ALL IN DANGER TOO!
WE KNOW!

THEY'RE *NUTS!*

BUT WE DON'T CARE!
ALL THAT MATTERS IS THAT WE CARRY OUT CHARON'S ORDERS!
HA HA HA HA HA

HARETA, STOP! WE NEED TO GET OUT OF HERE... NOW!
DASH
OUT OF HERE?
WHERE? HOW?!
TOO LATE! THERE'S NO TIME LEFT! WE'LL ALL BE BLOWN SKY HIGH TOGETHER!
NO...
WE'LL BE FINE.

SHIIIING
HEY! THE BOMB IS GLOWING!
IS IT ABOUT TO EXPLODE ?!
SHIIIING
KOYA!
NO. THAT'S LIGHT SCREEN.

WE'RE SURROUNDING THE BOMB WITH LIGHT SCREEN TO SOFTEN THE IMPACT!
SHIIIING
BUT THERE'S A *LIMIT* TO WHAT METAGROSS CAN DO...
I GET IT!
HEY, TRAINERS ...
LISTEN UP!
WE NEED YOUR HELP!
SURROUND THE BOMB WITH LIGHT SCREENS!

THRUMMMMM

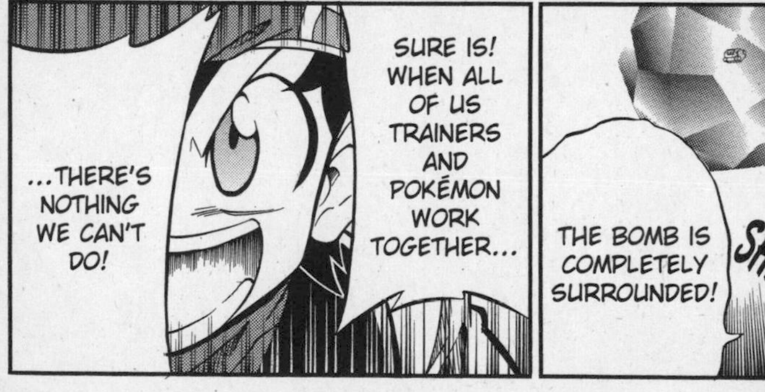
SURE IS! WHEN ALL OF US TRAINERS AND POKÉMON WORK TOGETHER...
...THERE'S NOTHING WE CAN'T DO!
THE BOMB IS COMPLETELY SURROUNDED!
WHA ...?!
SHRUUUUNG

KRA-KA-BOOOM
TAKE *THAT*, TEAM GALACTIC!

HWOOOOM

WHEW! WE *DID* IT! WE SAVED THE TOWN!
YOU DID IT, HARETA!

NOPE, IT WAS ALL KOYA'S IDEA. THANKS, BUDDY!

HARETA ...
YOU'VE GOT GREAT FRIENDS!
KAISEI!
JOLT
I'M INTERNATIONAL POLICE AGENT HANSOM!
JAB
AND YOU, KEISEI, ARE COMING WITH ME!
ARGH! NOT AGAIN!
I KEEP TELLING YOU, I DIDN'T DO ANY-THING!
RUSTLE
WELL, I GUESS ...
...I BETTER GET GOING!
!
LEAP

THUD
ARE YOU ON THE RUN, DAD?
YUP.
YOU'VE SURE GROWN UP, HARETA!
SHWK
HERE... A GIFT FROM MY TRAVELS!
RAISE IT WELL.
KAISEI!
GOTTA DASH. SEE YA, HARETA!
DASH
YOU WON'T GET AWAY THIS TIME! AFTER HIM, KOYA!

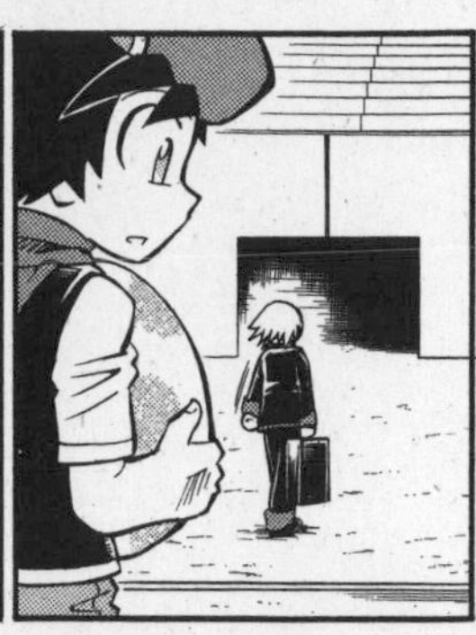
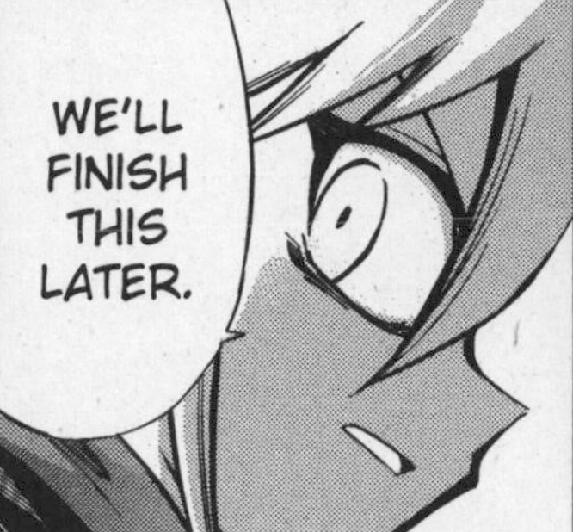
WE'LL FINISH THIS LATER.
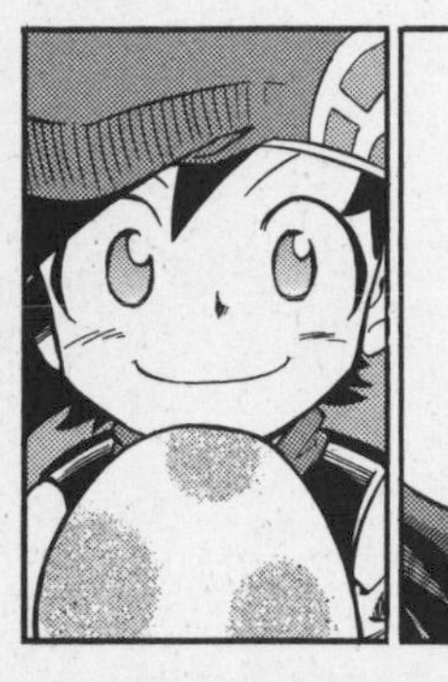
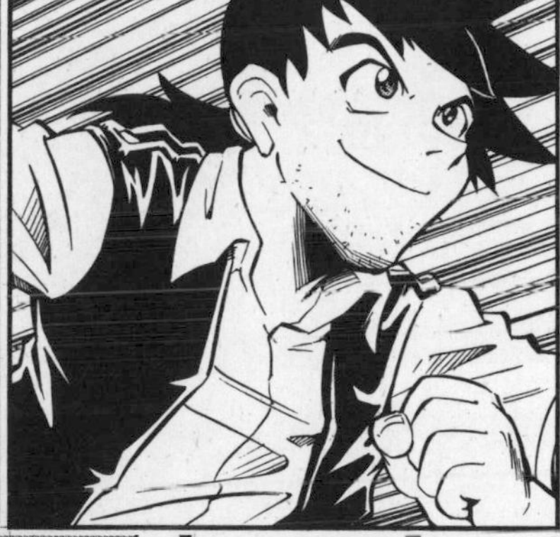
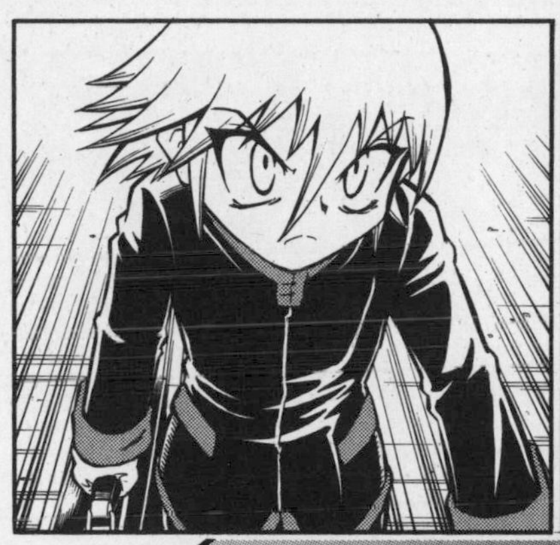

YOU BET! DAD... KOYA...

...SEE YA LATER!

CLICK

WUPPA WUPPA WUPPA

HEH HEH... SO...KAISEI IS ON THE RADAR AGAIN!

I'LL CAPTURE HIM MYSELF. HE'LL COME IN USEFUL...

I'LL TEAR THIS ***WORLD*** APART...AND GIRATINA TOO!

To Be Continued in Volume 7

I'M HANSOM!

POKÉMON DIAMOND
AND PEARL SPECIAL:
MITSUMI'S WISH

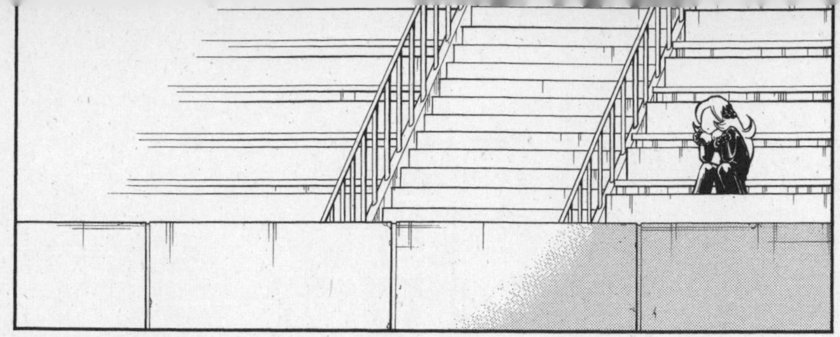

SIGH
WHAT'S WRONG? WHY IS THE CHAMPION, MS. CYNTHIA, LOOKING SO DOWN?

MITSUMI!
OVER HERE.
WELL, Y'SEE...

FIRST, I WAS REALLY LOOKING FORWARD TO OUR MATCH...AND YOU DITCHED IT. THEN THE TOURNAMENT GOT MESSED UP BY TEAM GALACTIC.

LICK SLURP

OOOPS

PLUS, HARETA LEFT. I'M BORED!

HARETA'S JUST TAKING A NAP, ACTUALLY...

...

TOSS

SO...

WANNA CONTINUE OUR POKÉMON BATTLE?

REALLY? YOU'D DO THAT FOR ME?

IT DOESN'T SEEM LIKE YOU ***WANT*** TO BATTLE ANYMORE.

BUT, MITSUMI...

YEAH... THAT'S SORTA TRUE.

I DON'T EVER WANT MY POKÉMON TO FACE THE KIND OF DARK BATTLES I PUT THEM THROUGH IN MY TEAM GALACTIC DAYS.

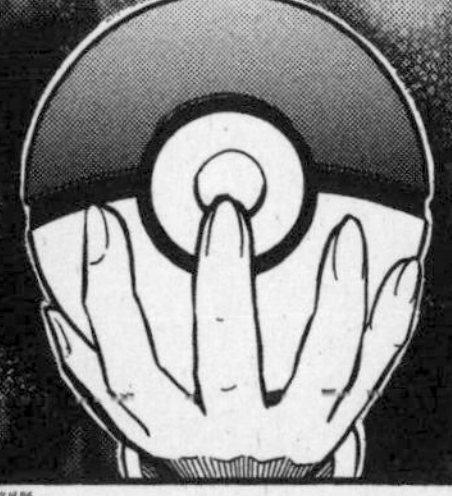

I WANT TO SHOW OFF THEIR ***GOOD*** SIDES IN POKÉMON CONTESTS.
I WANT EVERYONE TO SEE THEIR ***TRUE*** BEAUTY!

THAT DAY…
…I LEARNED THAT POKÉMON AREN'T WEAPONS FOR BATTLE… THEY'RE FRIENDS.

FRIENDS WE GET TO *SHARE* OUR BEST TIMES WITH!

I ALWAYS LOVE SEEING A POKÉMON EVOLVE. IT REMINDS ME HOW WE ALL...
...GROW, GETTING STRONGER AND TRANSFORMING INTO MORE BEAUTIFUL VERSIONS OF OURSELVES.
MITSUMI, YOU CAN TOO, YOU KNOW.
YOU CAN GROW OUT OF THE CURSE OF TEAM GALACTIC...
...AND TRANSFORM INTO SOMETHING NEW!

SPIN
OH, DON'T WORRY...
I CAN STILL CRUSH YOU IN BATTLE... FOR FUN.
THEM'S FIGHTIN' WORDS! ♡

SO... SHALL WE GET STARTED?
HOP
HWOOOO

POP

In the Next Volume

Hareta's father urges him to hurry up and find the legendary Pokémon Giratina. But someone else is on the trail! Then Cyrus goes missing. Is he in need of a rescue? Plus–a Pokémon is born!

Bonus Story: "Return to Hareta's Home Forest!"

Available July 2010!